The Adventures of Rufus O'Malley

'A NEWFOUND FRIEND'

Dear Reader
I hope you enjoyed this book
enough to leave a
splendid review on Amazon.
Many thanks
Philip Huzzey
Local Shropshire Author

Dear Reader
I hope you enjoyed this book
enough to leave a
splendid review on Amazon.
Many thanks
Philip Huzzey
Local Shropshire Author

The Adventures of Rufus O'Malley
Copyright © Philip Huzzey 2018 All Rights Reserved
The rights of Philip Huzzey to be identified as the author of this work have
been asserted in accordance with the Copyright, Designs and Patents Act 1988
All rights reserved. No part may be reproduced, adapted, stored in a retrieval
system or transmitted by any means, electronic, mechanical, photocopying, or
otherwise without the prior written permission of the author or publisher.
Spiderwize
Remus House
Coltsfoot Drive
Woodston
Peterborough
PE2 9BF
www.spiderwize.com
A CIP catalogue record for this book is available from the British Library.
The views expressed in this work are solely those of the author and do not
necessarily reflect the views of the publisher, and the publisher hereby
disclaims any responsibility for them.
All characters in this publication are fictitious and any resemblances to real
people either living or dead are purely coincidental.
ISBN: 978-1-911596-88-2
eBook ISBN: 978-1-911596-89-9

The Adventures of Rufus O'Malley

'A NEWFOUND FRIEND'

by
Philip Huzzey

SPIDERWIZE
Peterborough UK
2018

In memory of my mother and father, Shelia and Bert, my brother, Rodney John, and my mother and father in law, Pauline and Jim.

My dogs, Duke, Rufus and Bruno, who were true examples of man's best friend.

Lorraine and Olivia for being the best wife and daughter one could wish for.

I love you all.

About the Author

Philip Huzzey is an actor who has appeared on television and independent films. He has produced and directed his own feature length movie (Out of Gas) and is also a musician and songwriter who has now turned his hand to writing children's stories. Born in the Sussex village of Henfield, he now lives with his wife and daughter in Shropshire.

CONTENTS

Map of Zanimos and neighbouring countries designed and drawn by Philip Huzzey, with inclusions from Christopher Young, Lorraine Huzzey and Ali Smith.

INTRODUCTION

It is believed by some that far out in the depths of the universe, there are worlds just like ours that are inhabited, and I have it on good authority that there is a world where only animals live. How do I know this, you ask? Because I have been there! So let me take you on a magical journey, to a world that only exists in your wildest dreams; well, your dreams maybe, but not mine...

My story begins behind the great walls of the city of Ungerborg. Now, Ungerborg is a city that is made up of a low town and a high town, and they are separated by a stone bridge that spans the great river Olgen. Although it is the marketplace in the high town that is bustling with animals during the daytime, it is in the low town where most of the city dwellers live. The city mainly comprises of brick-built houses, apart from a baker's, a general store, and The Rosfarl Inn, which are all very old timbered buildings built long before the city walls were erected.

The high town is built on the top of a hill and is accessed by crossing the river bridge and walking up a steep cobbled causeway that leads through a tall archway. In times of trouble, the portcullis would be lowered, and no animals would be allowed in or out of the high town. Standing within the walls of the high town is a most beautiful castle, built of granite and marble, and it is here that the Boar King Rosfarl and his Queen, Rosia, sit on their thrones and govern the land of Unger. The castle, with its tall spires, towers and high walls seems to stretch out in all directions, watching over the kingdom.

The land of Unger has borders to several different countries and the city of Ungerborg has become a trading centre for travellers from far and wide who come to buy, sell or barter for goods and wares. They come from the great seas of the east, the frozen depths of the north, and only the brave or foolish come from the west; for they risk ambush from the bandits who live in the black forests of Arven, and death in the treacherous bogs of Moorsher. There is however no trade with the Nordeamian Empire situated to the North East of Unger as these two countries have had centuries of war between them, and although a truce exits, there is no trust between King Rosfarl and Emperor Porturios, a large black rat who rules Nordeamia. Fortunately there is a deep canyon that separates the two countries, and the only way to cross this is via a drawbridge on the Unger side

which remains open to prevent any
Nordeamian threat.

In fact, were it not for the
neighbouring land of Zanimos, the rat
army of Nordeamia would have overrun
Unger many years ago. Now Zanimos
lies to the south of Unger behind an
intimidating mountain range, and it
is well known to everyone that only a
native of Zanimos (a Zamosian) can
travel safely along the magical mountain
pass without fear for their life; of this
you will learn more later....

Welcome to the world of Rufus O'Malley

About Rufus

Rufus O'Malley is an Alaskan malamute.
He was born in the North of the World
and is descended from royal blood; in
fact, he is a Prince among malamutes,
but he seldom mentions this, as he
believes that all animals are equal.
Bestowed upon him by his father, Odana,
the King of the North of the World,
is the gift to use magical powers, and
he has sworn an oath only to use these
powers for the good of other animals.
He is strong and fearless, he has the
kindest of hearts, and he loves to roam
the world seeking adventures. He is also

very quick witted and sometimes uses mischievous methods to show naughty or bad animals the errors of their ways. When he comes to Zanimos, he falls in love with it and decides to stay. At least for a while…

About Zanimos
The land of Zanimos is situated on a peninsula and surrounded by the sea, apart from the north, where there is a mountain range called the Chameleon Mountains. Anyone wishing to enter Zanimos from this direction must travel along the Enchanted Pass, however, only a Zamosian can travel safely along the treacherous mountain pass without fear for their life, as the mountains and pass are protected by the magical spirits of wizards who lived in Zanimos hundreds of years ago.

Here are just some of the animals you will meet in Zanimos:

Hamilton

She is a hamster, who only recently moved to Zanimos from the land of Unger. Hamilton loves to invite her new friends to her cottage for afternoon tea and a chat.

Horace

A very friendly hare who is always polite, pleased to help, and is by nature a very fast runner.

Brodney

He is the owner of the Zanimos town general store. He is perceived by others as a rather grumpy and surly badger who is a tough street trader; however, he is honest, brave and reliable.

Papachuan (Pronounced Puppa chew one)

He is the Town Mayor, and he is a very clever and wise yellow labrador whom all animals go to when something troubles them. Many years ago, his forefathers came from the North of the World and settled in Zanimos.

Barnaby
A newfoundland dog who is extremely strong, an excellent swimmer and is devoted to his best friend Rufus O'Malley. Although he is not in this story he later travels to Zanimos and follows Rufus on many of his adventures. It transpires that Barnaby is also a cousin to Papachuan.

Chapter 1
In the City

Our story begins just as the market stalls were closing for the day. It was almost five o'clock, and hurrying along a narrow cobbled street just behind the market square was a smartly dressed red fox. He was wearing a tweed jacket, matching trousers and a green cravat around his neck, and he carried a brown leather brief case; he was in a hurry, and he glanced at his pocket watch, shaking his head as he did so. He reached an old grey stone building where the lower half of the windows were covered with bistro style curtains that hung from brass poles. He opened the solid oak door and stepped inside, closing the door behind him. A wooden sign above the door creaked on its metal hinges in the wake of a gentle breeze that blew along the street, and on it the words, Hamilton's House, Fine Teas and Cakes could be read.

Once inside, he was greeted by the smiling face of a golden hamster who showed him to an empty table. She was wearing a floral apron and stood over him holding a notepad and pencil, awaiting his order.

"And how are you today Sasha?" asked the hamster.

"Well, Hamilton, I have been very busy. So busy in fact that I almost forgot about me tea."

"Well it is nearly five o'clock; I was about to finish for the day."

Sasha looked disappointed.

"Don't worry my old friend, you can still have some tea. After all, you've always been a true friend, and you have offered me such a fair price for my lovely house."

This brought the smile back to Sasha's face, as he loved his afternoon tea at Hamilton's.

"Talking of your house, Hamilton, I've just come from the bank, and I've got your money. It's all here," said Sasha, tapping the front of his briefcase excitedly. Hamilton glanced around the room to take stock of who was there. She moved closer to Sasha and drew his attention to two scruffy looking weasels who were sitting at a corner table with their heads close together and whispering to one another.

"Shush, Sasha, we'll discuss this after I've closed up for the day and all the customers have left," she said in a quiet voice. "In the meantime, can I get you your usual?"

"Oh, yes please, and do tell me you still have some of your lovely chocolate cake left!"

"Only one piece I'm afraid, and I have

saved it for a rather special customer."

"Oh dear." Sasha's face dropped. "And who's that?" he asked.

"You, my dear young fox," she said with a smile.

"Why, you tease, Hamilton. Now just get along and get me my tea, and make it pronto!" said Sasha, in a playfully bossy voice.

Hamilton smiled and walked out towards the kitchen.

As she entered the kitchen, there in front of her on the round table that stood in the centre of the room was a wooden tea tray. And on the tray was a teapot, cup and saucer, sugar bowl, milk jug, knife, cake fork, a butter dish, a pot of strawberry jam and a pretty floral lace napkin. There was also one large warm scone and a gigantic portion of chocolate cake.

Hamilton's eyes opened wide and she gave a broad smile.

"Goodness me, you are marvellous,

Bloomsberry. One thing though, the tea is it –"

"Earl Grey, just as he likes it," replied Bloomsberry excitedly.

"You've thought of everything," said Hamilton, looking up at the smiling face of Bloomsberry rabbit, who was beaming with pride.

"Well, I've been here long enough to know the regular customers, and you could set your watch by Sasha, though he's a little late today."

"I'll tell you what, Bloomsberry, you take it to him."

Bloomsberry's face lit up even more.

"I'd love to."

Bloomsberry had been working in Hamilton's teahouse ever since she had arrived in Ungerborg many years ago. She had been born in the lands of the west, and after her parents had passed away she decided to go to Ungerborg to find work. She was a brave rabbit, and she had travelled through the black forests of Arven, where she had used her great speed to avoid capture by the bandits. She had also travelled unguided through the bogs of Moorsher without being lost or trapped by its treacherous bogs.

She was always a happy rabbit and a delight to be with, and being from the west she had a lovely softly drawn out accent.

While Bloomsberry took in the tray to Sasha, Hamilton peeped out between the curtains that separated the kitchen from the dining area and took a quick glance around at her customers. Although she had many regular customers, it was the strangers that fascinated her, and if she didn't find out their business by polite conversation, she liked to watch them and guess what they did for a living or why they were in Ungerborg. Although a lot of customers had left, as it was nearly closing time, there were still a

few animals for Hamilton to study.
There were two rather fat looking
boars, who between slurps of their
coffee were laughing very loudly.
They wore smart blue uniforms with
the royal crest upon their chests, and
leaning against the walls next to them
were their long pikes with pointed
metal heads; the weapons of the King's
soldiers. There was a smartly dressed
rabbit who wore glasses perched on
the end of his nose and held a small
notebook closely to his face. He was
muttering to himself and scribbling
away in his book.

He was a stranger to Hamilton,
probably a trader from afar who
was tallying up his sales of the day.
Trustworthy Sasha, as always, had
a napkin tucked into his cravat and
was sipping his tea in between taking
large bites of chocolate cake; his eyes
half closed as he savoured every bite.
The expression on his face always

brought a smile to both Hamilton and Bloomsberry.

The weasels were still there, cackling away in the corner. They would occasionally look up and take a shifty glance around the room, before putting their heads back together again.

Ghastly beasts those weasels, they do so give me the creeps, she thought, as a shiver ran down her back.

Suddenly a great sadness filled her heart, for it was to be her last day here in the teahouse that she had made so famous throughout the city. Here, where there were so many memories. Still she had worked hard for many years and had at last decided to move away into the country, and at least she had found the perfect buyer for the teahouse in Sasha. Hamilton was very fond of him and was thrilled when he asked Bloomsberry to stay on and work for him.

Having finished his tea, Charlie the old

border collie stood up and slid his chair underneath the table, which made a scraping noise on the floor. Charlie had a hardware store in the city that he had owned for many years, and he had been one of Hamilton's first customers. "Well ole girl, I'm sorry to see you go, but all the very best for your retirement," he said, bending down and giving Hamilton a gentle kiss on her cheek. Hamilton went a little red with embarrassment.

"Thank you for everything, Charlie," she said with a smile.

"And don't you let that Sasha get too bossy," he called out, looking back into the kitchen at Bloomsberry.

"I won't," said Bloomsberry with a smile. As he walked past Sasha, he gave the fox a friendly tap on the shoulder.

"See ya, Sasha."

"Take care, Charlie," replied Sasha with a mouthful of chocolate cake.

Charlie made his way towards the door,

but before he reached it, the door was opened and in stepped a large and rather surly looking badger.

He wore denim trousers and a black duffle coat, and he had a large green rucksack on his back. Everyone in the room looked over and took notice of the badger, and the weasels seemed particularly interested in him, especially after noticing the two pistols that were tucked under his black leather belt.

"Why, Brodney, come for Hamilton have you?" asked Charlie.

"That's right," came the gruff reply. Brodney had been one of Charlie's customers for many years, and it was Charlie who had told Hamilton that Brodney had a cottage for sale.

"And I see you're prepared for everything," said Charlie, looking at the two pistols.

"Can't be too careful," replied the badger in a gruff voice.

"No, that's true enough. There's always some scheming creature that'll try and rob ya."

"Let 'em try," replied Brodney with a scowl.

Charlie opened the door and looked back towards Hamilton.

"You'll be quite safe with this fellow, Hamilton," he said, tapping Brodney on the shoulder. "Cheerio!" he called out as he closed the door behind him.

"Fancy a cup of tea, Brodney, there's plenty in the pot?" asked Sasha, holding up the teapot.

"Don't mind if I do," grunted Brodney, removing his rucksack and sitting down at the table opposite Sasha.

"Let me get you both a fresh pot," interrupted Hamilton, and she promptly took the teapot from Sasha's paw and took it into the kitchen.

After all the customers had left , Bloomsberry bade farewell, and Sasha,

Hamilton and Brodney began to discuss their business transactions.

"Well then, Hamilton, here is your payment for the teahouse," began Sasha, tipping his briefcase up and letting its contents of gold coins fall carefully onto the table. "As we agreed, there are 300 gold coins."

Hamilton's and Brodney's faces lit up at the sight of them.

After staring at all the coins for a moment, Hamilton began to put them into piles of ten, and very soon she had stacked them all up and was counting them out.

"295, 96, 97, 98, 99, 300!" she exclaimed.

Sasha produced an official document and placed it in front of Hamilton.

"And here is the bill of sale for the teahouse. Just sign here and here," he asked, handing Hamilton a rather lovely blue patterned fountain pen. She took the pen and signed as requested.

"This is for you, and this is mine," said Sasha, handing Hamilton a copy of the bill of sale. Hamilton studied the document and realised that there was no going back now, and for a moment she looked rather sad.

Sasha could see by her expression that she was a little upset.

"It's what you want, isn't it? If not, I'll tear it up and take me coins back."

"Would you really, would you really do that, Sasha?"

"Of course I would, Hamilton, I know how much the place means to you," replied the fox with a kind smile.

"Oh, my dear Sasha, you are a true friend, but in my heart of hearts I know what I want. I've always dreamed of living in the country, and if Brodney's cottage is as lovely as he says, I just know I'll be very happy."

"It's the most beautiful cottage, the prettiest in the whole of Zanimos," uttered Brodney with pride.

"And when shall I pay you, Brodney?" asked Hamilton.

"Once we get to Zanimos and you're happy with the cottage, as I know you will be, I'll get the papers drawn up and you can pay me. You needn't pay me anything 'til then."

"Oh, Brodney, you are also a trusty fellow. How lucky I am to be dealing with such good and honest animals."

"I think it's time for a toast," said Sasha.

"How about a beer?" added Brodney.

"I've got some sherry. Will that do?" uttered Hamilton.

"Lovely," replied Sasha.

"Better than nothing I spose," grumbled Brodney.

Hamilton nipped off to the kitchen, and moments later she returned with a silver salver, on which were three glasses and a decanter full of sherry. She filled the three glasses and handed one glass to Brodney and one to Sasha before picking up the remaining one herself.

"To Hamilton! May she have a long and happy retirement!" said Sasha.

"'Ere 'ere," said Brodney.

With this, all three animals raised their glasses and promptly drank their contents.

"Oh, that was lovely, thank you," said Hamilton. "And Sasha, I would like to wish you well with your new venture."

"It can't fail, it simply can't fail. After all, I've got Bloomsberry to run the teahouse, and she's simply marvellous."

"Yes, she's a darling. I'll miss her."

Brodney stood up and took hold of his rucksack.

"Right, I'm off then," he said

"Going so soon, Brodney?" asked Sasha.

"I'm off to the Rosfarl Inn. I have a room there."

"And what time shall I see you tomorrow?" asked Hamilton.

"Six o'clock sharp. I'll bring a cart for

your things. I know it might
be early for you city folk Hamilton, but
we've got a long ways to go."
"Don't worry, I'll be up," she replied.
Sasha and Hamilton watched Brodney
disappear along the street.
"Brodney's not a great one for words, is
he?" said Hamilton.
Sasha laughed.
"No, he's not, but Charlie's found you a
true and honest badger, and from his
looks he won't stand any messing. He's
just the sort of person you want as a
companion on a long journey."
"Yes, I'll feel safe with him."
"Err, any chance of another sherry,
old girl?" asked Sasha, eyeing up the
decanter.
"Oh Sasha, you are awful," she replied,
filling their glasses once again, with a
glint in her eye as she did so.

Hamilton was so very excited about
moving to her new home in the country

that she hardly slept a wink, and she found herself getting up at four o'clock in the morning. Still, it gave her plenty of time to get those last-minute jobs done before Brodney arrived. While she was rushing around and getting things ready, she constantly kept an eye on the time, and sure enough, dead on six o'clock, Brodney arrived. He had brought with him a large hand cart on which to carry Hamilton's possessions.

"Mornin," he said, as he popped his head through the open door.

"And good morning to you, Brodney," called Hamilton as she reached the bottom of the stairs.

"Right, what you taking then?" he grunted.

Hamilton showed Brodney what she was taking with her, and he started to load her possessions onto the cart. Within a couple of hours, the cart was loaded. They were about to set off on their journey, when the words, "Hello, my dear," were uttered by a familiar voice, and on turning around Hamilton was greeted by the sight of her friend, Bloomsberry.

"Oh, Bloomsberry, you're just in time. Brodney and I were about to leave, and I was going to lock up and drop the key through the letterbox."

Bloomsberry looked puzzled.

"But if you had put the key through the letterbox, how was I to get in?"

"Oh…I gave Sasha all the other keys last night, and he said he would drop one off to you on his way home."

"Well, the silly ol' fox must have forgotten. In fact, I saw him pass my house last night, and he looked as happy as a sand boy and was singing away at the top of his voice."

Hamilton put her paw to her mouth and smiled.

"Silly old fox indeed, I think he went home last night feeling just a little bit tipsy."

Bloomsberry grinned. "The sherry?" she asked with a smile.

"Afraid so," replied Hamilton, and the two of them started to giggle.

"Speak of the Devil," uttered Brodney, looking at the familiar figure of Sasha, who was making his way towards the teahouse.

"Hello everyone!" called the fox as he reached his friends.

He looked towards Bloomsberry and waved a large key in the air.

"Sorry my dear, I meant to drop this off last night, but for one reason or another, it completely slipped my mind." Sasha stepped forward and handed Bloomsberry the key.

"Don't you worry yourself, Sasha, it's a wonder you found your way home after a glass of Hamilton's sherry," replied the rabbit with a cheeky grin.

"Oh, I think we managed more than one glass... didn't we Sasha?" added Hamilton with a smile.

"Well, maybe a couple," replied Sasha, grinning and raising his eyebrows.

"Right then, Hamilton, lets make the best of the early start," grunted the badger.

Hamilton and Bloomsberry embraced one another. "Oh I will miss you, dear Hamilton," sobbed Bloomsberry as she planted a kiss on Hamilton's cheek.

"And I will miss you," replied Hamilton, as a small tear ran down her face.

"Come on Hamilton," said Brodney, as he carefully lifted her onto the front of the cart.

Brodney nodded farewell to Sasha and Bloomsberry and started to pull the cart along the cobbled street.

"Bye bye!" said Hamilton, waving her paw.

"Take care!" called Bloomsberry.

"Keep in touch!" shouted Sasha.

"I will," replied Hamilton in a voice that was just about audible, as she was slightly choked with tears.

Sasha and Bloomsberry watched Brodney and Hamilton slowly make their way along the street and waved furiously until the two animals had disappeared from sight.

"Do you think we will ever see her again?" asked Bloomsberry, who was still sobbing and held a handkerchief to her eyes.

"You never know," replied Sasha, putting his paw around her shoulder. "Now come on old girl, let's have a nice cup of tea and some...crumpets?"

"Tea and crumpets coming up," she replied, wiping the tears from her face and stepping into the teahouse.

Sasha loitered for a moment and looked up at the wooden sign above the door.

"Hamilton's House, Fine Teas and Cakes...I think we'll keep that," he said to himself.

Chapter 2
Journey to Zanimos

Hamilton continued to wave until
Brodney had pulled the cart around the
corner at the end of the street and
they had entered the market square.
Although it was still early, there
was already a buzz of activity as the
shopkeepers and market traders were
preparing for the day ahead. As they
made their way through the square,
Hamilton bade farewell to many of her
old friends, including Charlie the collie,
who called out and waved from the
doorway of his shop at the far side of
the square. Once through the square,
they passed under the great archway
of the high town, where two royal

guards raised their pikes in a farewell
gesture. They descended the causeway
and crossed the bridge that led them
over the river Olgen and through the
houses of the low town.

They left the stone path of the city
behind and headed south along a grass
track that had little signs of use,
except for some light wheel marks,
as this was only used by those from
Zanimos and therefore not a busy
route. After half a mile or so, they
reached some woods, and Hamilton,
feeling that this was probably her
last chance to see Ungerborg, quickly
turned back to look at the city.

This grand metropolis had been her
lifelong home. It looked so safe and
strong with its walls and turrets, and
the beautiful shimmering towers of the
royal palace confirmed its importance.
Just for a moment, Hamilton was filled
with mixed and confused feelings;
she was, after all, leaving everything

she had ever known behind her, her friends and her teahouse. But, on the other hand, she was also very excited about moving into the countryside and realising her lifelong dream.

The badger, sensing her feelings began to put her mind at rest.

"Come on old girl, cheer up. After all, if you don't like me cottage, you can always come back you know."

"Thank you Brodney," she replied, trying to cheer up. "I'm sure I'll be fine, it's just...I've never been away from Ungerborg."

Underneath her nervousness, Hamilton wanted a new life in the countryside so very much, and the fact that it was finally happening had a soothing effect that made her begin to feel more positive and upbeat.

"Tell me, Brodney, how long will it take us to get to Zanimos?"

"We'll be there by tonight."

"Oh, I can't wait. From what you've told

me it sounds so very lovely."

"It is that, and there's space to breathe. You can keep your cities, give me Zanimos every time."

The track, which had been smooth and straight, now became more rough and uneven as it weaved its way around the trees, and as they went further into the woods, the sun struggled to shine through the canopy of branches and leaves. As they got deeper into the woods, there were places where the sun beams shone through the tall trees, casting long dark shadows that moved as a gentle breeze blew the branches back and forth. Hamilton didn't like the darkness of the woods or the creaking noises the trees made as they moved with the wind, and to calm her nerves she began humming a tune to herself. In the distance, several birds could be heard talking to one another. Their sounds were short and sharp, more like a whistle than a tuneful song. Being a

city dweller, Hamilton didn't often hear
birds in chorus.

"Oh, how lovely. Birds singing," she said
out loud.

"Umm," grunted Brodney, seemingly
deep in thought.

The noisy birds were now getting
closer to them, and Hamilton turned
around and scanned the woods behind
her, eagerly hoping to get a glimpse
of them; but there was no sign of the
birds.

"Brodney, what sort of birds are they?"
she asked excitedly.

"The kind that spell trouble!"

And with this, he started to pull the
cart as fast as he could.

Hamilton immediately felt frightened.

"Brodney, Brodney, what's wrong?!" she
cried.

"Got to get to that glade, we'll be safer
there," he replied, breathing quickly.

"But what is it?"

"Vermin, that's what. Now, hold on

tight, and whatever you do, don't get off the cart!"

Hamilton was scared beyond belief. Though she didn't know what she was scared of, she knew that Brodney was running from something or someone, and if a big strong badger was running away, what on Earth could he be running from? She felt cold from fear now, and she held herself tightly, tucking her head into her shoulders.

Brodney was pulling the cart as fast as he could, and the rough track with its ruts and bumps caused it to rock and shake. Hamilton had to hold on as tightly as she could to avoid falling off. Her heart was beating faster now, and her eyes were moving from side to side, as she anxiously awaited the appearance of this demon. Brodney reached the glade and brought the cart to an abrupt halt. Hamilton could feel the warmth of the sunshine now, but she felt no less frightened, Brodney paused for a moment to catch his breath, but on hearing movement in the long grass a short distance in front, he quickly moved away from the cart, and within moments out stepped a grisly, evil looking weasel. He wore a metal helmet on his head, chainmail adorned his body, and he brandished a sword that shone in the sunshine.

"We know you, badger," uttered the weasel, pointing his sword at Brodney.

"Yeah, we do, don't we," came a second cackling voice.

"Oh dear!" exclaimed Hamilton, as she saw the other weasel standing behind the cart. He too had a sword that he waved in the air, and his sharp yellow teeth could be seen as he snarled and snorted.

Brodney turned back to the first weasel.

"And I know you...Belius," growled Brodney.

Belius walked slowly towards Brodney,

holding his sword outright.

"Hand over the money, and we spares you and the hamster," he said, laughing through his teeth and pointing his sword towards Hamilton.

"No!" uttered Brodney in a gruff voice.

"Hand it over," continued the other weasel, bringing his sword down hard on the side of the cart, which made Hamilton jump.

"Can't we give them just a little money... to make them go away," said Hamilton in a frightened tone.

"We give 'em nothing," growled Brodney defiantly.

"Then you knows what you'll get," said Belius, raising his sword in the air and charging towards the badger. He screamed as he raced forward.

"Ahhhhhhh!"

Brodney moved quickly. He reached inside his jacket, pulled out his pistols, and pointed them towards the weasel.

"Stop, or I'll fire!"

Belius paused for a moment, but his greed was far greater than his fear of the guns, and he foolishly continued his charge.

Brodney squeezed the triggers of both guns and they fired simultaneously, causing such a roar that Hamilton put her paws to her ears. The weasel knew he'd made the wrong decision as he felt the metal balls impact upon his chest, and even though the chainmail prevented them from entering his skin, their force was enough to cause him great pain and to knock him off his feet.

"Ow!" cried Belius as his body hit the floor with a thud.

Knowing that he had immobilised the first weasel, Brodney turned around to deal with the second one, who was now just a few feet from Hamilton with his sword raised and ready to strike. Brodney acted quickly. He pulled a large dagger from inside his jacket and stepped forward to intercept the weasel. But the weasel saw him coming, raised his sword above his head and swung it down towards Brodney's body. The badger stepped backwards to avoid the blow. Swoosh went the blade as it cut through the air. But instead of meeting its target, it struck the ground and became embedded in the soil.

"Blast, blast!" snarled the weasel as he fought to free his sword.

But he was too slow. Brodney stepped forward, held his dagger against the weasel's throat and took the sword from his hand.

"Take your friend and leave us be, lest you forfeit your life," growled Brodney, pressing his dagger firmly against the weasel's skin.

"Alright, alright! Now let go, you're hurting my arm!" snapped the weasel. Brodney released the weasel and followed him over to Belius, who was still on the ground holding his chest.

"Help me up, Gritch," snapped Belius at

the other weasel, who quickly obeyed. Belius stared at Brodney, and as he snarled under his breath he reached down to pick up his sword.

"Oh no you don't. That stays with me," said Brodney firmly.

Belius looked up at the badger, bared his teeth and dropped his sword to the ground. He wanted to kill him, but he was too hurt to fight him now. The weasel and the badger looked at one another, growling as they did so, for both animals were fearless warriors who would fight to the death if necessary.

"One day, badger. One day your time will come," said Belius.

"Maybe. But not today."

"If I were you, badger, I would be very careful the next time you travel to Ungerborg, for you may find more than two weasels waiting for you."

"And if I were you, Belius, I would tread very carefully, for if word of this

deed should reach King Rosfarl…it'll
be off with your heads!" shouted the
badger. "Now, on your way, and keep to
the main path where I can see ya!"
Belius and Gritch made their way back
along the road to Ungerborg, and
with every step he took, Belius felt
a burning pain in his chest where the
metal shot had bruised him. And every
time he felt the pain, he vowed revenge
on the badger.
Brodney watched the weasels make
their way along the road until they
had disappeared out of sight. He then
walked around to the front of the
cart. He was just about to take hold
of the handles when he heard sobbing
from behind. It was Hamilton. She was
holding a small handkerchief to her
face and patting the tears from under
her eyes.
"There, there, it's alright now, the
nasty weasels have gone," began
Brodney with a reassuring smile.

"Oh, Brodney, I have never been so scared in all my life. I felt certain we would die," replied Hamilton in a most shaky voice.

"Well, it's all over, and you're quite safe now."

"Thanks to you."

"All part of the service," he said with a smile.

"But you risked your life, Brodney."

Brodney put a strong paw gently on Hamilton's shoulders and looked at her with a serious expression.

"Would you rather have let those vagabonds have all your money and forfeit your new life in Zanimos? No, of course you wouldn't. I've heard all about that Belius and how ruthless he is, and when I saw him and the other weasel in your teahouse yesterday, I knew he was up to no good."

"Oh Brodney, you're so brave, so very brave,"

Just for a moment, the badger started

to blush with embarrassment, and he afforded himself a modest smile.

"And Mrs Badger will be so proud of you, won't she?" continued Hamilton. Brodney quickly wiped the smile from his face, for he knew that his wife would be worried sick if she heard he had been fighting.

"Mrs Badger...oh yes, but it's best if we don't tell her about the weasels. She'll only worry, you know."

Hamilton smiled. "It will be our little secret, Brodney."

The badger cleared his throat and assumed his more typically brusque and proud manner. For although underneath his tough exterior was a heart of gold, he felt if he showed it too much he would be taken advantage of, especially as he was known as a tough animal to bargain with by the traders of Ungerborg and the animals of Zanimos.

"Let's be on our way then. We must get through the mountains while there's still daylight. The path's too treacherous to walk at night."

As these words left his mouth, he took hold of the cart by its handles and set off at a fast pace. Soon they were out of the woods and travelling across the open plains, from which they could see the mountains of Zanimos in the distance.

It was nearly six o'clock in the evening when Brodney reached the far side of the plains and began to climb a rocky path, which led through a small copse of trees that nestled against the foot of the mountains.

But these trees, with their long, needle shaped leaves, were different to the oak trees of the woods of Ungerborg. They were in fact pine trees. And on seeing them, Brodney's spirits lifted immediately, for he knew that in just a short time they would reach the mountains that formed the border between the realm of Unger and the land of Zanimos.

"At last, my homeland," he whispered to himself.

"Hamilton, we're nearly there!" He cried out excitedly.

But there was no reply.

"Hamilton!" he called, louder this time, but there was still no reply.

Brodney turned and looked over his shoulder and saw Hamilton yawning and stretching her arms.

"Oh, I am sorry, I must have dropped off," she began, holding a paw to her mouth.

"We're here, Hamilton."

"Here, where's here?"

"The Chameleon Mountains," replied Brodney with enthusiasm.

"The Chameleon Mountains! You do know your way through alright, don't you Brodney? Only I've heard stories of travellers getting lost in these mountains," she said, sounding uneasy.

"Lost and never found again," added

Brodney with a wicked tone of humour.
"Please don't tease, Brodney," she said,
sounding rather panicky.

"Don't worry, I've travelled through
these mountains since I was a boy,
when my father used to bring me
to Ungerborg," he replied, trying to
reassure her.

"And you've never got lost?"

"Never."

Brodney's breathing quickened now, as
he had to work harder to pull the cart
up the slope. But he was a tenacious
animal, and he made his way up through
the trees without stopping once for
breath. The path levelled out when
they had passed through the trees, and
Hamilton looked on in awe, as for the
first time she saw what the mountains
looked like close up. She could hardly
believe her eyes when she realised how
tall the high peaks of the mountains
were as they towered over her.

Apart from the odd slope, which was

crimson in colour, the mountains were
a very vivid blue, and Hamilton thought
that even the marble and granite
walls of the royal palace of Ungerborg
paled in comparison to these beautiful
mountains. While her eyes darted
back and forth, trying to take in all
the breath-taking landscape, Brodney
pulled the cart onto a wooden bridge
that led over a gorge, and as they made
their way along it, both of them began
to hear a booming and rumbling sound
that got louder the further they went
across the bridge.

"Brodney, what is it, what's that noise?"
asked Hamilton nervously.

"Look down there, me dear," he replied,
looking over the side of the bridge.
Hamilton peered cautiously over the
side of the cart and looked down below.
She had hardly taken in the view of the
formidable mountains when her senses
were bombarded with yet more new and
exciting experiences. She watched in

amazement at the raging torrent, the white water gushing and thundering as it crashed over the rocks.

She watched it fall to a pool below, where it hissed and bubbled and then flowed on downstream, meandering around the mountains before disappearing out of sight.

"It's spectacular, I've never seen anything like it before. But where does it come from, and where does it go?" she asked excitedly.

"It's from hundreds of springs, right here in the mountains, and luckily for us it goes all the way through Zanimos before it reaches the sea," replied the badger, as he pulled the cart off the bridge.

They were now getting closer to the mountain path, and to reach this they had to pass between two large rocks that jutted out from the base of the mountains. Hamilton thought that these were quite odd looking rocks, for they

were strange shapes that seemed
to peer out at them. But as she got
closer, these peculiar looking stones
began to form into discernable figures
that appeared to have been purposely
sculpted out of the rock. The two
shapes seemed to look at one another
across the path and were very similar in
appearance. They had long pointed hats,
long pleated gowns and they had faces
of strange beings that Hamilton had
never seen before.

Each sculpture had two strange looking
paws that were pointing over the pass,
and it looked as if they were trying to
touch one another. Their faces were
similar, but their expressions were
quite different. One of them had a
very stern and powerful face, while the
other exuded a much more pleasant
and forgiving countenance. Their size
also impressed Hamilton, as both
them were several times larger than
even Brodney, and the majesty and

reverence of the sculptures made her
feel quite insignificant in comparison to
them. Brodney stopped the cart before
reaching the sculptures and walked on
towards them alone. Hamilton felt a
little nervous being left on her own and
called out to him.

"Where are you going Brodney?"

"Just to make me peace with the
wizards."

"Wizards!"

Brodney turned around to her and put
his paw to his mouth.

"Shush," he uttered quietly under his
breath.

Hamilton looked on in disbelief as
Brodney began whispering to the two
strange rock figures. He only spoke for
a moment, and then he bowed to them
both before returning to Hamilton.
Hamilton thought the badger's behaviour
was extremely strange, but nevertheless
she was most intrigued by it all, and was
ready to spring her questions on him as

soon as he returned to the cart.

"What on Earth was that all about, Brodney? Why were you talking to those strange looking rocks?" she asked in an inquisitive tone.

"Ah, well...you see, if we're to have a safe journey through the mountains, we have to travel along the Enchanted Pass," replied the Badger, starting to pull the cart once more.

The thought of anything enchanted filled Hamilton with a mixture of nervousness and excitement all at the same time.

"Enchanted Pass," she uttered with a worried expression.

"Aye that's right. The pass is enchanted, and it's all the work of the wizards."

"Wizards! Where are they?" said Hamilton, with a worried expression on her face.

Brodney scratched his head for a moment.

"Well, it's difficult to explain really. Oh…if only I'd studied my history more when I was a young badger."

"Please tell me?" begged Hamilton.

"Don't know much to be honest," sighed the badger. "But you ask Papachuan, he knows all about the history of Zanimos."

"Papachuan, who's he?"

"He's our Town Mayor."

"Oh, I see...but can't you tell me anything, Brodney?"

"I know this much," began the badger, still scratching his head. "Hundreds of years ago, a wizard and his wife ruled over Zanimos. They looked after all the animals, and nobody wanted for anything. They even saved Zanimos from an army of invading rats."

"Rats, how awful!" she replied, cringing as she spoke.

"Awful ain't the word; rats is vicious, and ruthless!" exclaimed Brodney. "But the wizards sorted them out alright," he continued.

"What did they do?" asked Hamilton, sounding a little excited.

"Well, as I said, this here pass is known as the Enchanted Pass, and that's because of a spell the wizards cast that stopped the rats getting into Zanimos; oh, there were a few who did get through alright, but they were soon dealt with."

"And where are the wizards now?"

"Oh, they died many years ago, but their spirits live on, here in the mountains. So you see, they still watch over the land of Zanimos and the Enchanted Pass."

"My goodness!"

Brodney could sense that Hamilton was still a little worried.

"Don't you worry, we'll be safe. The wizards won't play tricks on an animal from Zanimos."

"Yes, but what about me? I'm not from Zanimos," came a nervous reply.

"Ah, but I am, and you're a good and

true animal, and the wizards will know that."

Hamilton still didn't look too convinced.

"Now, stop worrying. Mortuleez and Julianna will give us a safe passage."

"Who are they?" asked Hamilton.

"He's Mortuleez," replied Brodney, pointing to the stern and powerful face of the sculpture on their left.

"And that's Julianna, who was his wife," added Brodney, nodding his head toward the more pleasant looking face that looked opposite Mortuleez.

"So they were the wizards?" asked Hamilton.

"Well, we call em wizards, but Julianna was a witch of course."

"A witch!" exclaimed Hamilton, open mouthed. "But I've heard that witches are evil and wicked," she continued sounding very agitated.

Brodney laughed.

"Ah, you're thinking of black magic and powers of darkness you are."

Hamilton felt a shiver run down her back.

"Well, I don't know about black magic, but I've heard stories. You know, terrible stories, from animals who've been in my teahouse, and everything they said about witches was horrible, absolutely horrible."

"Ah, those are black witches. Now Julianna, she was a white witch. And as the story goes, a kinder witch you could never wish to meet."

"What's a white witch?" asked Hamilton, looking puzzled.

"White are good and black aren't, that's all there is to it," he grunted.

"I see," said Hamilton.

"Anyway, I always stop and say a few words to them, just before I enter the mountains. My father used to, and he always got home safely. That's why I do it, and I've always got home too."

"But they look so strange, like no animal I've ever seen," said Hamilton, looking

back at them with a puzzled expression.
Brodney laughed.

"What's so funny?" asked the hamster.

"They're not animals, they're called humans."

Hamilton contorted her face into a confused expression.

"Humans, what are they?"

"Oh, ask Papachuan, we've still got a long way to go," snapped the badger. He had got rather fed up with this bombardment of questions now, especially as he was having to work hard to pull the cart over some bumpy stones. And as he struggled on with the cart, Hamilton could hear him grumbling under his breath that he didn't know everything, and that he wasn't a blooming library.

Hamilton was initially shocked by this curtness from Brodney, but when she realised how much effort he was putting into pulling the cart along this rough stony track, she understood and instantly forgave him.

But she thought it was wise not to ask him any more questions about witches and wizards, so she settled down to enjoy the journey through the beautiful mountains. She was still a little bit nervous, but she had gained tremendous confidence in Brodney's ability to deal with anything that might befall them, so much so that she soon fell fast asleep, only to be woken several hours later as they arrived at her new cottage.

Hamilton had never seen anything so lovely in her life, and she fell in love with it instantly. Her face was a picture of joy, and all of the doubts in her mind were gone the moment she set eyes on the cottage.

"Oh, it is beautiful, so beautiful, Brodney. And it has leaded windows! You didn't tell me it had leaded windows, oh how delightful," she said, holding her paws and squeezing herself with happiness.

"Knew you'd like it," said Brodney with a beaming smile.

"Oh I do, I do!"

"Here, you let yourself in while I start to unload the cart," he added.

Hamilton took a large black key from Brodney's paw and proceeded to unlock the front door. She stepped into the hall, and after pausing for a moment, her excitement got the better of her and she hurried from room to room, trying to take in every last detail of the cottage as fast as she could.

"Where do you want this, Hamilton?" called out Brodney, holding up a wooden hat stand.

Hamilton ran down the stairs and pointed to a space on the hall floor.

"Just here, please," she said excitedly.

It was nearly dark when Brodney pulled the empty cart along the lane that lead

back to Zanimos Town and Hamilton
settled into her cottage
for the night. It was the end of a long
day, and it was the first night for
Hamilton in her new home. As darkness
fell, she watched the great Chameleon
Mountains that formed the backdrop to
the land of Zanimos gradually succumb
to the black of night and disappear.
I wouldn't want to be out in those
mountains at this time, she thought
to herself, as she drew her bedroom
curtains closed.

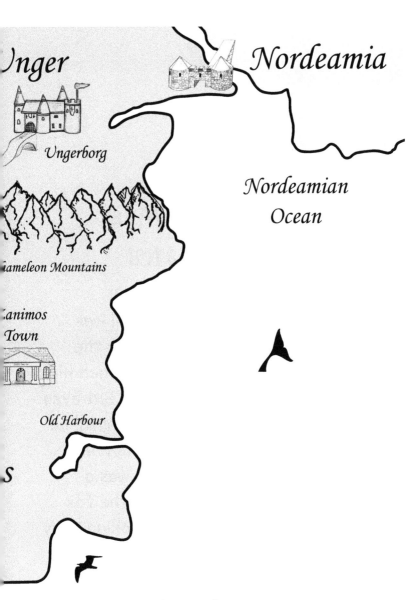

Unger

Nordeamia

Ungerborg

Nordeamian
Ocean

Chameleon Mountains

Zanimos
Town

Old Harbour

Zamosian Sea

Chapter 3
The Spirits Meet
Their Match

Later, in the depth of night, all was
quiet in the mountains, save for the
hooting of an owl that was perched high
up on a branch in a pine copse. But even
he was silent when he saw an animal he
had never seen the likes of trotting
calmly through the trees. It was a
large animal, far bigger than the fox
or badger, with a powerful looking body
and short pointed ears, and its tail was
plumed and carried over its back. The
animal's fur was a mixture of black and
white, with some grey. It had a large
mouth, its eyes were alert and fearless,
and the whole demeanour of the beast

was one of pride and majesty. The owl watched it trot up the slope towards the mountains, and as his curiosity got the better of him, he flapped his wings and followed the beast across the footbridge, which led over the river towards the mountains.

He tried to be as quiet as he could and kept his distance, but as the beast reached the two stone sculptures, it stopped in its tracks.

"Nice evening, Mr Owl," said the beast under his breath, still looking straight ahead. The owl was taken quite by surprise, for he was quite sure the beast hadn't seen or heard him.

"Yes, it is," he stuttered.

"Coming with me, are you? I would be glad of some company," continued the beast, turning his head and smiling.

"No, not me. I…I'll not fly through those mountains at night," replied the owl, as he turned and flew back to his pine copse. The beast watched the owl as it disappeared out of sight before turning around and studying the two stone sculptures for a moment, and then he continued on his way.

He followed the path, which wound its way around the mountains. The only sound for company was the burbling river that seemed to twist and turn in sympathy with the path. After about an hour, the two parted company. The noise of the fast flowing white water faded away as the path ran through a narrow gorge that cut its way between two of the highest peaks of the mountain range. At the far side of the gorge, the path seemed to twist and turn sharply and then dip into a sea of mist before disappearing.

Now, most animals would have been too worried to proceed, but the beast kept on trotting along, completely unaffected by the dense green mist that started to surround it.

Further and further he went into the

mist, and the further he went the thicker it got, but this did not seem to bother this animal, who nonchalantly continued on his way. Suddenly the silence was broken by a ghoulish howling and moaning, and although nothing could be seen due to the mist, it was obvious to the beast that some strange forces were present. The beast calmly sat on his hind legs and moved his head from side to side as if to search for the cause of these cries. He then took a deep breath and, moving himself around in a complete circle, he blew, and he blew, and he blew. In fact, he created such a fierce wind that the mist disappeared. He then sat perfectly still.

He was relaxed, yet alert and ready for anything. He then began to study his new surroundings, for the path was now in the middle of a pine forest. His senses were all charged; he was prepared for anything. The noises that

had been heard before started again.
Quietly at first, but getting louder
all the time, and these noises were
accompanied by strange shapes and
silhouettes that could be seen darting
amongst the trees and moving towards
him. They came right up close to him
and then darted away again. They were
nothing that could be touched or felt;
they were in fact from the spirit world.
They moved around the beast and
encircled it, and with their wailing
sounds and unearthly shapes they
sought to frighten and torment it.
The spirits were being mischievous.
Protecting Zanimos is what they had
always done, especially when they were
wizards, and they had done such a
good job that no strangers had dared
to enter the country for many years.
As a result, most days drifted on into
the next with nothing exciting ever
happening, but at last an uninvited
animal had entered their domain and

they were going to thoroughly enjoy themselves scaring it back to Unger. But this animal was different, and they could feel a strange aura surrounding it like nothing else they had encountered before. For instead of cowering with fear for his life, he simply remained still and looked on quite indifferently. They could sense that the beast had a great inner strength, and courage too, and they could feel his goodness. And there was something else, perhaps even magical about him. But spirits do not like meeting their match, and so they continued their onslaught in an attempt to frighten him. But this only served to annoy him, and he slowly began to bare his teeth; his large, sharp teeth. He then started to bark and snap at the ghostly apparitions, which caused them to flinch away from him. His barking became louder and louder until it even eclipsed that of the wailing spirits. It then turned into a continuous

howling noise, so loud and so full of
anger, that the spirits became so
frightened that they turned tail and
disappeared. The beast held his head
up and looked around; he smiled for
a moment and then let out a couple
of barks to congratulate himself for
scaring off the spirits. He then set off,
following the path, which had begun to
slope downwards, right to the end of
the forest, and as he left the woodland
behind, he could make out the shapes
of buildings in the distance below. To
the west of these was a large lake that
glistened under the stars. He felt the
sudden urge to run now, and he began
to trot. The trot turned into a canter,
and the canter a gallop, and with
speed that perhaps no other animal
could match he raced down towards
the settlement below. He covered
the ground between the wood and the
buildings in no time at all, and in an
instant he was walking over a humped

bridge that took the path over a river. He followed this for only a short while before finding himself standing in a cobblestone square where he stopped to take in the beauty of the picturesque town that surrounded it. As he studied the buildings around the square, the beast felt that this was a friendly and happy place, and although all the inhabitants were tucked up in bed for the night, he could somehow sense that it was a place where good animals lived. It was clean and tidy, and the buildings, which were mainly constructed of various colours of sandstone, were charming. Some were red, and some were cream, and the florist's, the public house and baker's were all pale yellow. On one side of the square was a pond, which was fed by a stream that came from the lake, and between the pond and the lake was a tailor's, a public house called The Wizards, and at the far

side of a narrow wooden footbridge
that led over the stream was a bank.
Next to the bank was a most imposing
building that stood out from all the
others as it was larger and taller. It
was constructed differently as well;
instead of sandstone, this building was
made of large white bricks, and at the
front of it were three rows of steps
that led up to a large solid wooden
door. Etched into the wall above it
were the words, Zanimos Town Hall.
At either side of the door were two
large marble pillars, which supported
a grand and ornate looking porch that
seemed to add importance to the
building. In comparison to the sturdy
walls, the tiled roof looked buckled
and warped, and was clearly in need of
some urgent repair work. As the beast
glanced around the square, he could see
some other shops, and one in particular
grabbed his attention: it looked like a
general store and above the entrance

had a sign with a badger's head on it.
The beast turned and looked along the
street that headed eastwards between
the newsagent's and the greengrocer's,
where he could see a small triangle
of grass. Beyond this was a red brick
building that was public library, and
further along the street were quainter
looking shops and buildings. The beast
trotted onwards, following a path
that took him southwards between
the baker's and newsagent's, where he
paused and looked back into the town.
"What a lovely little place this is.
Simply charming," he said to himself
with a smile. "I think I'll take a good
look around the countryside tomorrow,
but first I'll find somewhere to have a
little nap."
The beast then opened his large mouth
and had a long yawn.
It had been a long day. In fact, it had
been one of many long days, for the
beast had travelled from lands afar.

Chapter 4
A New Friend
for Hamilton

Early the next morning, as the sun began to beam out across the countryside, Hamilton could be seen beating the dust from a carpet that was hanging over a washing line. She had woken up full of enthusiasm and was giving her new home a well-deserved spring-cleaning. As she stood back from the carpet to allow the dust to settle, she heard some movement in the hedgerow at the front of her garden.

"Who is it?" she cried out nervously. "I know someone's there!"

After some rustling in the undergrowth, a furry animal with long ears and powerful hind legs leapt out of the bushes, and stood in front of her twitching its nose. It was a large brown hare. Hamilton was startled for a moment, but she had no need to be frightened as it was a friendly hare.

"Hello, my name's Nimblefoot. Horace Nimblefoot," he said with a smile, and held out a paw.

"And I am Hamilton Smythe," she replied, shaking it.

"Pleased to meet you, Hamilton, but what are you doing here? This cottage has been empty for years!" said the hare, as he sat down and began scratching an itch on his tummy.

"Why, I live here, Horace."

"Really, so Brodney's sold the cottage at last!"

"You know Brodney, do you?" she asked.

Horace smiled. "Oh yes, everyone in Zanimos knows Brodney. He's a bit of a surly old devil, but his heart is in the right place."

"And he's brave and strong, and he fought off two nasty weasels," replied Hamilton excitedly.

"Weasels! Where on Earth were they?" exclaimed Horace, sounding alarmed.

"They attacked us in the woods, not too far from Ungerborg."

"Ungerborg, the great city in the land of Unger!" said Horace in an excited tone of voice.

"Yes, that's right. I used to live there."

"How wonderful, I've heard such exciting stories about it. But I never get to go anywhere exciting," he replied, sounding slightly glum.

"You mean you've never been out of Zanimos?"

"Never."

"Not even into the mountains?"

"Well, once when I was younger, my father did take me to the edge of the mountains for a picnic, but that's as far as I've ever been. But you, Hamilton, you're so lucky to have travelled through the mountains."

"Yes, I know I am, Horace, and the sights along the pass, well, they were breath-taking. And the mountains were the most beautiful shade of blue I have ever seen," she said, grinning with excitement.

The hare smiled.

"Blue," he chuckled, pointing towards the mountain range in the distance. Hamilton turned around to look at the mountains, and she was so astonished when she laid eyes on them that she let out a gasp of breath.

"My goodness me, I can hardly believe my eyes!" she exclaimed, shaking her head in disbelief. "Why, they were blue, a beautiful deep blue when I travelled through them yesterday, and now they are green. "Tell me, Horace, what trickery is this, are my eyes deceiving me?"

Horace smiled. "No, dear Hamilton, they are not. You see, the mountains have the spirits and souls of the wizards who lived here hundreds of years ago, and they change colour whenever they want to. Sometimes they may not change for weeks or months on end, but occasionally they even change several times a day."

"I think that's so very spooky, to think that mountains have spirits," replied Hamilton.

"Oh, and there's more," began the hare in an excited tone of voice.

"More?" replied Hamilton, feeling slightly uneasy.

"Yes. You see, Hamilton, the wizards also act as guardians over the mountain pass."

"Oh yes, I've heard about that from Brodney."

"Ah, but did he tell you what the spirits can actually do, especially to strangers to Zanimos who dare to travel through them?"

"Not exactly," she replied with a frown. Horace moved a little closer to her and opened his eyes as wide as he could. He then began to speak in a very serious tone of voice.

"The spirits will play tricks on them, Hamilton, and if necessary they start to manipulate the mountain pass. They can make it change direction, or even divide it into many different paths, and they can even make it appear to crumble away in front of your very own eyes, leaving a deep chasm in its place. Oh, and they can draw a thick mist from the ground, a mist so dense that you cannot see. And they can make shrieking sounds, and ghostly shapes that are so horrible and frightening that no one could possibly stand them!" Horace didn't realise that Hamilton found this all rather too frightening; he was, after all, only trying to make it sound more enthralling. But whenever his voice sounded more serious she started to feel even more uneasy.

"Oh yes, you mark my words, Hamilton," continued Horace in a very dramatic tone of voice. "Any stranger to Zanimos who walks along the Enchanted Pass will be so frightened that they will soon run back to Unger with their tail between their legs."

"Oh dear," replied Hamilton, playing with her whiskers, as hamsters do when they feel frightened or worried. "But isn't it possible for any strangers to get through the mountains?" she asked timidly.

"Well, it's never happened as far as I know, at least not in my lifetime. And anyway, if anything dangerous were to get through the pass, the mountains would warn us," he replied in a reassuring tone.

"Warn us, how would they do that?" asked Hamilton.

"Why, by their colour, my dear." On seeing the puzzled look on

Hamilton's face, Horace continued to explain.

"*Listen, there's an old Zamosian rhyme, it goes something like this.*

When mountain shades be warm or bright, all will be peaceful, no trouble in sight. But when colours of fire have set them alight, animals of Zanimos prepare ye to fight."

So you see, Hamilton, if ever the mountains appear to be on fire, then look out for your life, as trouble is afoot."

All this had unsettled the little hamster, and Horace, sensing that Hamilton was feeling a little uneasy, put his arm around her shoulder.

"Now, don't worry old girl, you made it alright didn't you," he said, smiling softly.

Hamilton nodded her head. "But if I had known all about this magic and wizardry, I don't think I'd have left Ungerborg."

"Now, don't be silly, Hamilton, you were

quite safe, after all you had Brodney to guide you here."

Hamilton smiled, feeling a little less worried now.

"You know, whenever I go into Brodney's store, he always tells me about his visits to Ungerborg. I know all about the Rosfarl Inn where he stays, and about this delightful teahouse where they serve the most delicious chocolate cake."

"A delightful teahouse, a delicious slice of chocolate cake! Oh, how kind of him." A beaming smile quickly crept across her face.

Horace was quiet for a moment, as if deep in thought.

"Now I've got it," he exclaimed, waving a paw in the air excitedly. "Brodney told me, it was called Hamilton's Teahouse! Yours?" he continued with a smile.

"That's right," said Hamilton, feeling full of pride.

"And it was in my teahouse that

Brodney told me he was selling this cottage, and when he described it to me I instantly fell in love with it."

"Yes, it's such a lovely cottage," replied Horace, admiring the pretty pink plastered walls, the old oak woodwork and the ivy-covered chimney, which had a funny twist to it just below the bright red chimney pots.

"But what became of your lovely teahouse, Hamilton?"

"I had to sell it to buy this cottage, Horace."

"And you don't miss living in Ungerborg?" asked Horace.

"Well, I only arrived yesterday, so it's too soon to say yet, but I simply adore the countryside. Mind you, I think I will miss making tea and cakes and chatting to my customers," she replied, sounding rather sad. But after a moment, Hamilton's face lit up and she became rather excited.

"I know, Horace, would you like to come

in and have some tea and cakes?"
Horace studied Hamilton's expectant
expression and knew there was only one
answer to give.

"Oh, that would be nice, very nice". He
replied, with a broad grin on his face.
"And I can tell you more of my journey,
and how bravely Brodney fought off
the horrible weasels."

"Oh, yes please," replied Horace
excitedly.

Once inside Hamilton's cottage, the
two new friends set about preparing
their tea. While Hamilton was busy in
the kitchen, Horace was in the parlour.
First of all, he laid Hamilton's pretty
lace cloth over the table, and then
placed some mats on top of it, and
after he had finished this he began to
help Hamilton carry the food out into
the parlour. Horace couldn't believe his
eyes when he caught sight of all the
food that Hamilton had prepared.

"Yummy yummy!" he exclaimed, rubbing his tummy with glee and feasting his eyes on the food. There were cheese sandwiches, cucumber sandwiches, cheese and tomato sandwiches, various homemade cakes and a gigantic chocolate cake.

While the two of them were going to and fro the kitchen and parlour, Hamilton started to notice some of the food disappearing. First it was some cheese sandwiches, then some cucumber sandwiches and then several of her homemade cakes.

"Oh Horace!" began Hamilton sharply, "Why can't you wait until we sit down at the table before you start to eat?"

"But I haven't eaten anything!" he exclaimed, sounding rather confused.

Hamilton stood with her hands on her hips and began to tell him off.

"It's one thing to take food from the plates behind my back, that's just greediness, but quite another to tell lies," she said.

Horace pricked up his ears and stared at her in amazement.

"Oh, Hamilton how could you say such nasty things? Why, I haven't touched a morsel, and I always tell the truth." Hamilton glared at Horace, lifted her nose in the air, and stormed off into the kitchen to fetch some napkins, muttering to herself as she went.

Horace turned and called out after her. "I don't tell lies, and it's very unfair of you to say I do. And, what's more, I'm your guest and you are not treating me at all politely!"

"That's because you're a bad hare, Horace!" she snapped, brushing past him. But as she entered the parlour, Hamilton let out a loud scream and dropped all the napkins onto the floor. On hearing her scream, Horace froze for a moment. Then, fearing something terrible had happened, he dashed into the parlour, where he saw Hamilton standing as still as a statue and staring out of the window.

Chapter 5
Rufus Makes his Entrance

The two animals, looking at each other with fear in their eyes, jumped into one another's arms, and stood shaking in the centre of the parlour.

Because there in front of them, with its head poking through the open window, was the most terrible and frightening sight. It was a huge beast with a long nose and pointed ears, and as it chomped on a large piece of chocolate cake, its sharp white teeth could be seen. When it saw the two animals huddled together, it finished the cake in a single gulp and licked its lips with a bright red tongue.

"Oh dear, I'm sorry to startle you. And

I do apologise for eating your delicious food, so please allow me to pay for it," said the beast.

The beast looked to the animals for a reply, but they were far too scared to speak. "I insist," he continued, and as the words left his mouth he held out a massive paw, and as if by magic, he plucked a shiny gold coin out of the air. He offered the coin to the animals, but they were far too terrified to take it. "Come, come little creatures, there's no need to be frightened," he said, placing the coin on the table. But Horace and Hamilton remained huddled together, too frightened to move, let alone speak. "I don't bite, you know," continued the beast, licking a piece of chocolate cake from the end of his nose. Horace was the first to speak and swallowed deeply before he began.

"But you eat little animals, don't you?" he asked in a frightened voice that was barely audible. The beast gave a chuckle and then started to clean between his teeth with his long sharp claws.

"Oh, Mr Wolf," pleaded Horace. "Please don't eat us, we're not very tasty, and I'm sure you'd rather eat some more sandwiches and chocolate cake instead of us."

The beast tilted his head backwards and opened his huge mouth, showing those large sharp teeth once more, and Horace and Hamilton closed their eyes and held each other as tightly as they could, each fearing that they were to be eaten. For a moment, all was silent, and then the beast began to roar with laughter.

"Ha ha, ha ha, ha ha," he laughed, shaking his head from side to side as he did so.

Horace and Hamilton slowly opened their eyes, and when they saw the beast laughing to himself they glanced at one another in disbelief.

Feeling a little braver now, Hamilton began to speak.

"Why are you laughing, Mr Wolf?" she asked, still holding tightly onto Horace.

"Mr Wolf indeed. Why, I am no such thing," he replied with a frown.

His expression became more serious now, which only served to make Horace and Hamilton more agitated. "Tell me, do you have wolves in this country of yours?" he asked in a sombre tone.

"No, not anymore," replied Horace shaking his head, "but they did live here, hundreds of years ago."

"Good. Nasty things, wolves. Some you can trust, but most of them spell treachery," replied the beast.

"Then, you're not a wolf?" uttered Horace so nervously that his teeth began to chatter.

"A wolf, no. You'll know the difference if you ever come to face to face with one, believe me...I'm a malamute, an Alaskan malamute, and my name is

Rufus O'Malley," he replied, holding his head up with pride.

The beast then smiled, and looked firstly at Horace and then at Hamilton. As he looked deeply into their eyes, their bodies began to feel warm and safe, and a sensation of goodness and kindness swept through them, which banished the fear they had felt from him. They had no control over this sudden change of mood, and they couldn't and didn't want to fight it.

It was inexplicable, but Rufus was an extraordinary animal, and he had made them feel so relaxed and at ease that they couldn't help but smile at him.

"And now my new friends, perhaps you'll tell me your names," said Rufus in a cheerful tone.

"Well, I'm Horace. Horace Nibblefoot. And this is Hamilton Smythe," uttered the hare.

"And I am very pleased to meet you both," replied Rufus.

"Does this mean you're not going to eat us?" asked Horace.

"Of course not," replied Rufus, laughing. "I don't eat animals, I prefer to make friends with them; at least the good ones that is."

"Well, my dear," began Horace, looking at Hamilton, "wouldn't it be nice to ask Mr O'Malley to tea?

Hamilton smiled and nodded in agreement.

"Please, Mr O'Malley, do stay and have tea with us?" she asked.

"We've got plenty of food," added Horace.

Rufus gave a large smile. "Of course, I'd love to. I've travelled a long, long way, and I'm really quite hungry. That's why I couldn't resist your lovely food."

"I understand," uttered Hamilton.

Rufus turned to Horace and put a large paw on his shoulder.

"I'm sorry if I got you the blame for eating the food," he said, looking towards Hamilton and raising his eyebrows as if to make her feel guilty for chastising Horace. Hamilton saw the expression on Rufus's face and suddenly realised how wrong she had been in thinking that Horace had eaten the food.

"Oh, Horace, please forgive me, I'm sorry for being so rude and nasty to you," said Hamilton gently squeezing him.

"Oh, that's alright; it's all sorted now isn't it. But I was slightly tempted you know," replied Horace.

"And I don't blame you. After all, the food is delicious," added Rufus with a broad grin.

After Hamilton had made some more sandwiches and cakes, she brought in a lovely pot of piping hot tea and called her two new friends to the table. Horace couldn't wait to tuck into the food, but as soon as he began to eat, a thought suddenly occurred to him.

"Mr O'Malley," he began.

"Just call me Rufus," replied the malamute.

"Well then, Rufus, I was just wondering," continued Horace with his mouth full of a cheese and tomato sandwich.

"Horace!" exclaimed Hamilton, giving him a look of disapproval as he tried to talk and eat at the same time. Horace, looking slightly embarrassed, quickly finished his sandwich, while Rufus, who found it all quite amusing, quietly chuckled to himself.

"Sorry," began Horace. "Now, where was I...oh yes.

How did you get into Zanimos Rufus, did you come by sea?"

But before Rufus could reply, Hamilton interrupted.

"Or did you come through the Chameleon Mountains, along the Enchanted Pass?" she asked enthusiastically.

"I did come through some mountains, and along a rather twisty path," replied Rufus.

Horace and Hamilton turned and looked at one another in disbelief.

"I really don't understand it," said Horace, shaking his head.

"Understand what?" said Rufus.

"Well, if you will beg my pardon, I don't understand how you, an animal who is not from Zanimos, could make it safely through the Enchanted Pass."

Rufus raised his eyebrows and smiled.

"Weren't you at all frightened?" asked Horace.

"Frightened, frightened of what?" replied the malamute.

"Why, the spirits that live in the mountains and protect Zanimos," replied Horace.

"They're the spirits of wizards," added Hamilton.

"Oh, that is rather clever," uttered Rufus, who didn't seem at all bothered about wizards or magic spirits.

Horace was about to explain further, but an excited Hamilton beat him to it.

"You see, Rufus, the wizards watch over the pass, and if you're not from Zanimos, their spirits will start to play tricks on you."

Hamilton was speaking as though she had lived in Zanimos for years instead of only a few days, and Horace couldn't help but laugh to himself.

"Isn't that right, Horace?" she continued.

"Yes, that's right. But how did you escape the wizards' magic, Rufus?" asked Horace, scratching his head.

The malamute slowly smiled at the animals.

"I met your spirits alright, so have no fear about your wizards' magic, it still works."

Horace drew a sharp intake of breath.

"You met the wizards' spirits?" he uttered quietly.

"Well, I didn't meet them in the sense of the word; I saw them, I heard them, and I even felt their presence."

"You could hear the spirits?" asked Horace in disbelief.

"One only has to listen, dear boy," answered Rufus.

"But what did they say?" exclaimed Hamilton, rather excitedly.

"And what did they look like?" added Horace.

The two excited animals then began to bombard Rufus with questions, and for a moment or two he couldn't get a word in. Finally, he raised his paws and gestured to the pair of them to stop.

"Quiet, quiet, please be quiet and I will tell you," he uttered in a very commanding tone, and the two animals were immediately silent. "Firstly, they didn't speak with words like animals, but you could feel their thoughts as they flowed around you. And they could sense if you were good or evil, fearless or afraid, and they could look deep into your soul," he said, moving his eyes back and forth from Hamilton to Horace. "And as for their appearance, they were like nothing else in this world. Their shapes were ghostly and transparent, and all you could feel was a chill in your bones as they brushed up against you."

"Oh don't, you're frightening me," said Hamilton.

"And me too," said Horace.

Rufus gently took hold of the two animals with his large paws and began to speak in a soft tone of voice to reassure them.

"Just remember, if you've got a pure heart and are not frightened, you will normally find that spirits will let you be."

He then smiled at them and they began to feel much less worried.

"Do you mean that you've met magic

spirits before?" asked Hamilton.
Rufus smiled.

"On my adventures I've seen many strange and wonderful things."

"Would you tell us about your adventures?" asked Horace.

"As long they're not too frightening," added Hamilton, twitching her whiskers.

"Please, please," continued Horace enthusiastically.

"Alright, alright," replied Rufus, and Horace's face lit up with excitement.

"But let's have our tea first, shall we. After all, I don't want to talk with my mouth full, do I," added Rufus, smiling at Horace.

"No," replied Horace, with an embarrassed expression.

The three new friends then started to feast upon the lovely spread that Hamilton had provided. And as Rufus turned around to peer out of the window and admire the lovely view of the Chameleon Mountains, Horace leant over to Hamilton and whispered in her ear.

"I wonder if Rufus knows any magic. I didn't see where he got that gold coin from, did you?" he said, speaking as quietly as he could.

Hamilton put a finger to her mouth.

"Shush, he might hear you," she replied. Now, malamutes have very good hearing, and Rufus's was exceptional, and as he turned around to face them he had a slight grin on his face, as he had heard everything.

"Ready for my stories then?" he said, rubbing his large paws together. The two animals nodded their heads in reply and sat up to attention. Rufus then began to tell the little animals many of his adventures, and no sooner had he finished telling one story than they would beg him to tell another one. His stories took them to far away countries, and they learnt about strange animals, of kings and queens and beautiful palaces, and of dark lands and evil monsters. Horace, who was normally a chatterbox, was captivated by the stories, and he didn't utter one word of interruption. Hamilton, on the other hand, was enjoying the stories, but she would grip hold of Horace and snuggle up to him whenever there was anything that frightened her.

When Rufus had finished his last story, Horace incessantly asked all sorts of questions, while Hamilton, who had found some of the stories a little too scary, only asked the odd one or two.

"Oh, I wish we could have some adventures, don't you Hamilton?" uttered Horace.

"I think I've had enough adventures for the time being," she replied, referring to her journey to Zanimos and the attack by the weasels.

"Well, I'd love an adventure. Nothing exciting ever happens to me," said

Horace, looking despondent.

Rufus studied Horace's expression for a moment. He had seen it all before; faces lighting up with enthusiasm at the thought of having a marvellous adventure, and then looking miserable at the true prospect of it never happening at all. And Horace, with his face resting on his paws, did look particularly glum.

"Horace," began Rufus, with a warm smile. "You never know what's around the corner, you might find adventure at any time, and my advice to you is don't go looking for it. It will happen if it's meant to. I'm always having adventures. It's as if they seem to follow me around, and they usually happen when I'm least expecting it."

He paused for a moment, looking back and forth at Horace and Hamilton, and his smile widened. "You know, I think I'll stick around for a while; and who knows, one might just follow me here..."

LOOK OUT FOR RUFUS IN
HIS NEXT ADVENTURE
'MONTY SAVES THE DAY'

Milton Keynes UK
Ingram Content Group UK Ltd.
UKHW020632050924
1512UKWH00054B/519